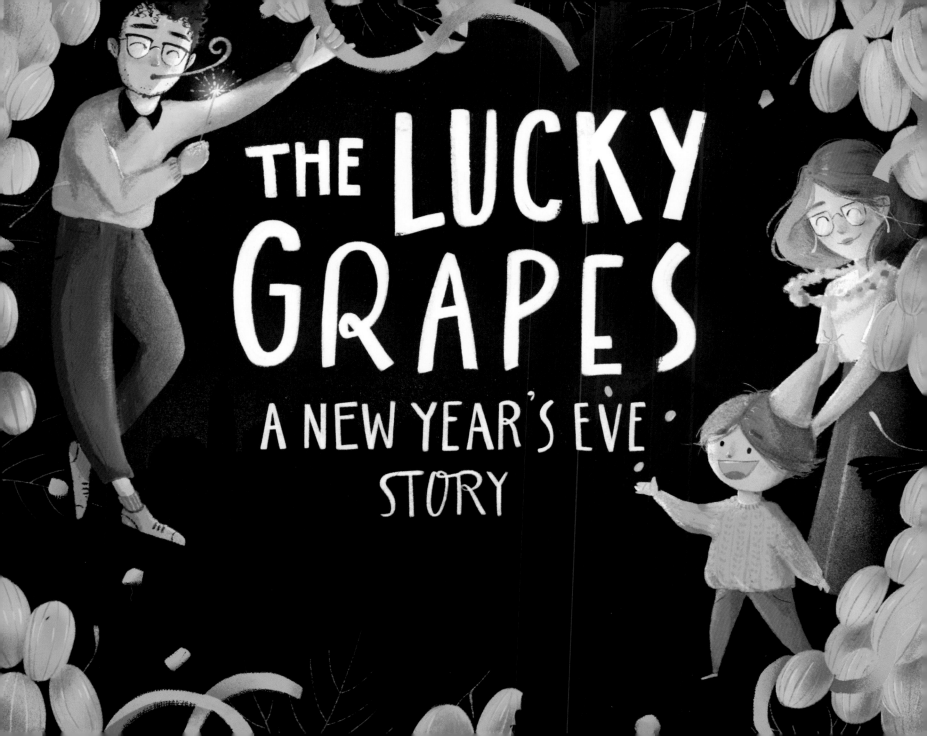

THE LUCKY GRAPES

A NEW YEAR'S EVE STORY

For my nephew Ethan, who eats grapes every day. —TK

To my parents Pili and Rafa, and to my family who, year after year, share the lucky grapes with me. —MA

Sky Pony Press books may be purchased in bulk at special discounts for sales promotion, corporate gifts, fund-raising, or educational purposes. Special editions can also be created to specifications. For details, contact the Special Sales Department, Sky Pony Press, 307 West 36th Street, 11th Floor, New York, NY 10018 or info@skyhorsepublishing.com.

Sky Pony® is a registered trademark of Skyhorse Publishing, Inc.®, a Delaware corporation.

Visit our website at www.skyponypress.com.

10 9 8 7 6 5 4 3 2 1

Manufactured in China, May 2022

This product conforms to CPSIA 2008

Library of Congress Cataloging-in-Publication Data is available on file.

Cover design & illustration by Marina Astudillo

Edited by Nicole Frail

Print ISBN: 978-1-5107-6888-8
Ebook ISBN: 978-1-5107-6889-5

THE LUCKY GRAPES

A NEW YEAR'S EVE STORY

Written by
Tracey Kyle

Illustrated by
Marina Astudillo

SKY PONY PRESS

Sky Pony Press
New York

Tonight there is a **celebración** for New Year's Eve.
Rafa has been counting down the hours 'til they leave.

Mami says he's old enough to finally stay up late.
Papi says the plaza has a show that's worth the wait.

DING DONG! Rafa jumps. Everyone is here!
The family has gathered for the last day of the year.
Tío cries, "**¡SORPRESA!** Tiny grapes without the seeds!"
"Perfect!" Mami smiles. "This is just what Rafa needs."

"Also sliced and peeled," Tío says. "And extra sweet."
Mami hugs him. "**Gracias**, Tío. Safe enough to eat!"

"**¡Uvas!**" Rafa shouts, but Mami moves them out of sight,
warning they are lucky grapes, only for tonight.

Tío says at midnight, they'll listen for the chimes.
Everyone will eat a grape, one-by-one, twelve times.

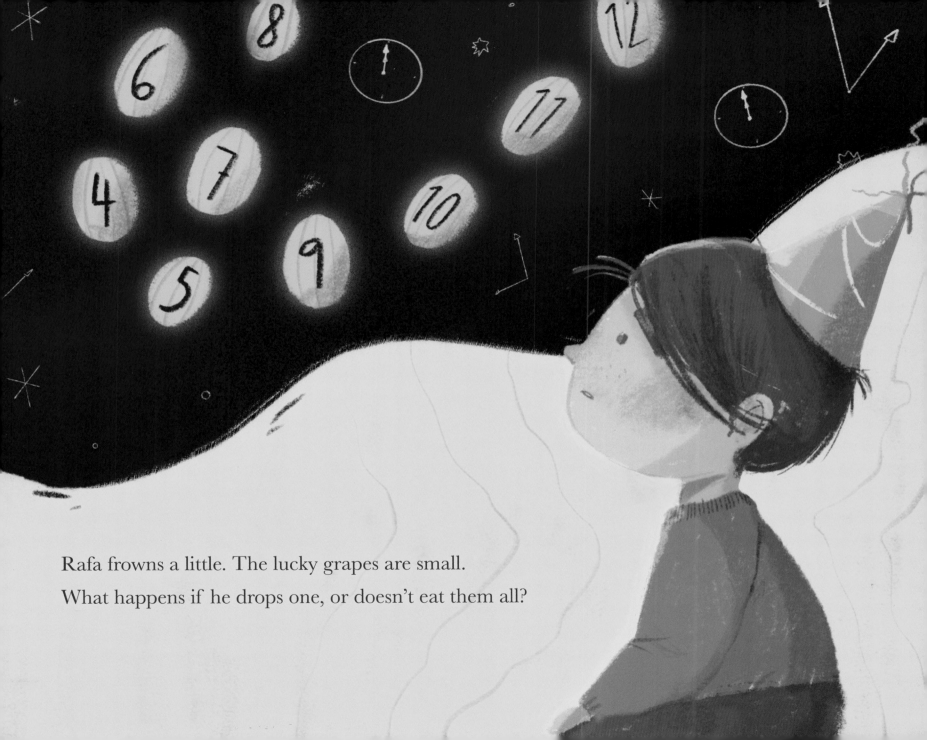

Rafa frowns a little. The lucky grapes are small.

What happens if he drops one, or doesn't eat them all?

"**Nada**," Mami tells him. "The **uvas** are tradition."
Papi claims the "lucky" part is only superstition.

Tío laughs and disagrees. "Rafa, you can do it.
I can carry extra grapes. Together we'll get through it."

Rafa yawns. It's getting late. He has to stay awake!
This lucky grape tradition means the new year is at stake.

Papi puts out **tapas**, tiny plates of yummy snacks.
Mami tells the family to catch up and relax.

Garlic shrimp. Figs with ham. Salty, fried **almendras**.
Tío can't stop eating. "These are ¡tapas **estupendas!**"

Dinner is a fancy feast of roasted fish and peas,
fried croquettes, **ensalada**, crusty bread and cheese.

After dinner, Rafa yawns. He needs a long **siesta**.
But if he falls asleep he'll miss the lucky grape **fiesta**.

Tío gets him moving. "Let's pack the grapes in bags."
"Tío, I can count them! I can do it!" Rafa brags.

Rafa knows his numbers well. **"Uno. Dos. Tres."**
He places each grape in the bag. **"¡Cuatro. Cinco. Seis!"**

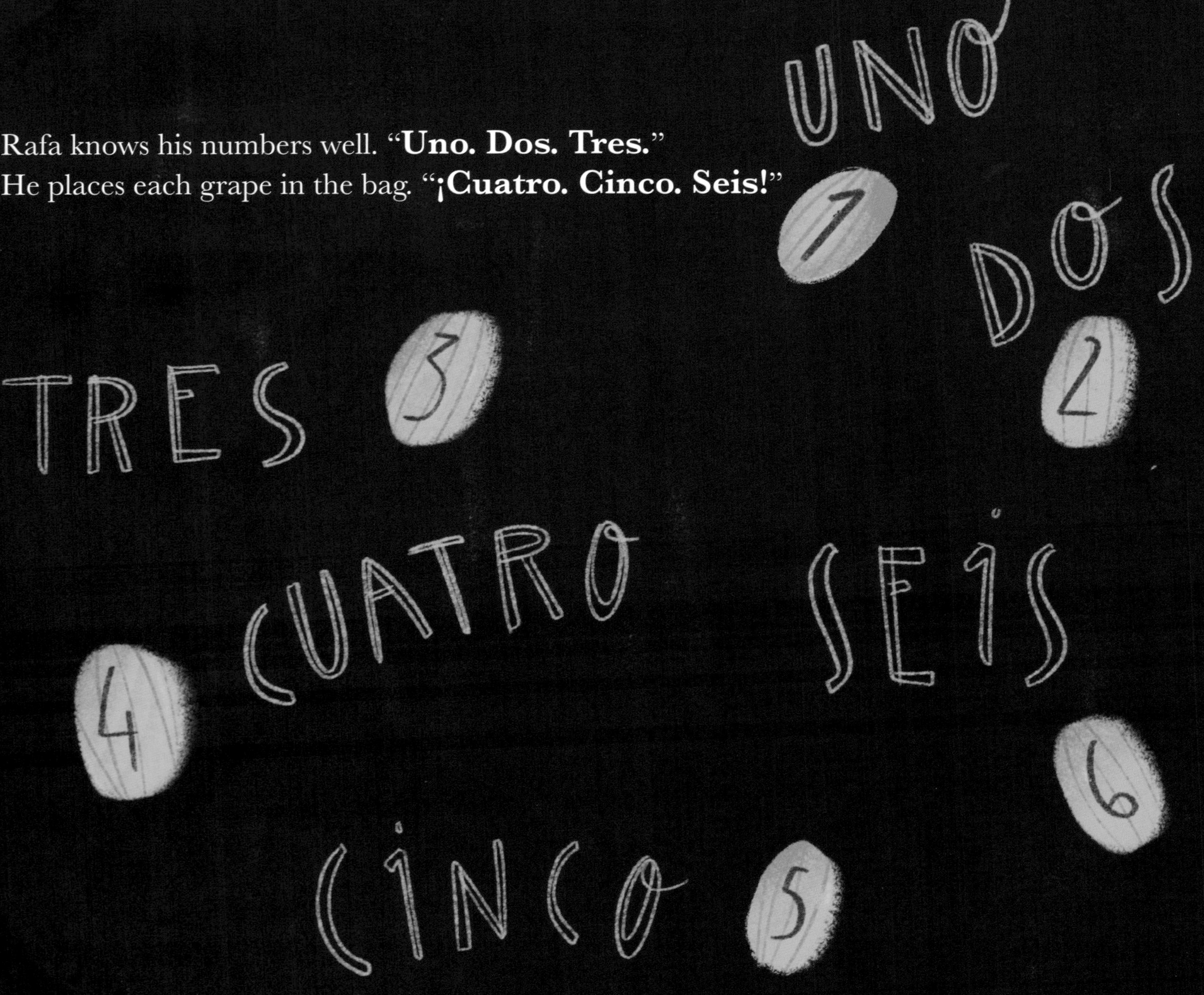

UNO

DOS

TRES

CUATRO

SEIS

CINCO

SIETE 7

OCHO 8

NUEVE 9

DIEZ 10

ONCE 11

DOCE 12

"**Siete, ocho, nueve.**" He counts the grapes with glee.
"**Diez, once, doce.** I'm done! This bag's for me!"

"**¡Bravo!**" Tío hollers. Rafa asks, "Can I count more?"
Mami says to pack more bags. "For us, too, **¡por favor!**"

Midnight is approaching. They dress up and they go, strolling to the plaza, the lucky grapes in tow.

The city streets are buzzing. Rafa eyes the scene. **Niños** to **abuelos** and all ages in-between.

Merry music mixes with the honking horns of cars. Up ahead, the plaza sparkles underneath the stars.

Tío turns to Rafa. "I doubt you're tired now!"
Partygoers pack the plaza. Rafa utters, "WOW . . ."

Blanketed by winter air, they join the huddled crowd.
Singing. Whistling. Reminiscing. New Year's Eve is loud!

Papi places Rafa on his shoulders. "Hold steady!
Listen for the warning bells. Then, GET READY!"

Staring at the ticking clock with pure exhiliration,
Rafa joins the countdown as they start the celebration.

Ding, dong, ding, dong, ding, dong, ding.
Rafa eats the lucky grapes. One for every ring.

¡FELIZ AÑO NUEVO! Fireworks, non-stop!
BOOM! BANG! ZOOM! HISS! CRACKLE! WHOOSH! POP!

Lit up like a glow stick as he soaks up the display,
Rafa joins his family. They hug and shout, **¡OLÉ!**

Rafa throws confetti. And yet he can't believe
he's nestled in the plaza celebrating New Year's Eve.

Rafa yawns a little, but still he beams with joy.
He stayed up late. He ate the grapes. He's such a lucky boy.

NUMBERS 1 TO 12 IN SPANISH

1	UNO	OO-NOH		7	SIETE	See-EH-teh
2	DOS	DOHS		8	OCHO	OH-choh
3	TRES	TREHS		9	NUEVE	Noo-WEH-beh
4	CUATRO	KWAH-troh		10	DIEZ	Dee-EHS
5	CINCO	SEENG-koh		11	ONCE	UHN-seh
6	SEIS	SEH-ees		12	DOCE	DOH-seh

GLOSSARY (in order of appearance)

SPANISH WORD	ENGLISH MEANING	PRONUNCIATION
Celebración	Celebration	seh - leh - brah - cee - OHN
¡sorpresa!	Surprise!	Sohr - PREH - sah
Uvas	Grapes	OO - bahs
Nada	Nothing	NAH - thah
Tapas	A hot or cold appetizer or snack in Spanish cousine	TAH - pahs
Almendras	Almonds	Ahl - MEHN - drahs
Estupendas	Amazing	Eh - stoo - PEHN - dahs
Ensalada	Salad	En - sah - LAH - dah
Siesta	Nap	See - EH - stah
Fiesta	Party	Fee - EH - stah
¡Bravo!	Bravo!	BRAH - voh
Por favor	Please	POORfah - BOHR
Niños	Children	NEE - nyohs
Abuelos	Grandparents	Ah - BWEH - lohs
¡Feliz año nuevo!	Happy New Year!	Feh - LEECE AHN - yoh noo - EH - loh
¡Olé!	Hooray!	Oh - LEH

AUTHOR'S NOTE

A typical Nochevieja (New Year's Eve) party in Spain shares plenty of similarities with the celebrations we have here in the United States: dinner with family and friends, the countdown at midnight with noisemakers and confetti, and staying up into the wee hours of the morning. But the most traditional ritual of the Spanish Nochevieja is las doce uvas de la suerte, the "twelve lucky grapes."

Many Spaniards will head to the local plaza to celebrate, but others choose to stay home and watch the festivities on TV. Madrid's famed Puerta del Sol hosts the grandest fiesta and is similar to the gathering at New York's Times Square. As midnight approaches, there are warning bells called "the fourths," or los cuartos. Then, there are twelve chimes, las campanadas, one for each month of the new year. The goal is to eat all 12 grapes so you'll have good luck each month. The most popular grapes are small, peeled, white, and seedless.

You can even find these special grapes already packaged at the supermarket! Many parents, however, will choose to give young children raisins, berries, or even the uvas gominolas (gummy grapes) sold in stores.

There are two theories as to how this tradition began. The first dates back to 1880, when upper-class Spaniards imitated the French by celebrating the New Year with grapes and wine. This led to the general population bringing grapes to the plaza in Puerta del Sol as a way to imitate—or make fun of—the rich. The second theory proposes that in 1909, the grape producers in Alicante (a region in southwest Spain) had a surplus of white grapes and designed a creative way to sell them, leading to the moniker of "the lucky grapes."

¡Feliz Año Nuevo!

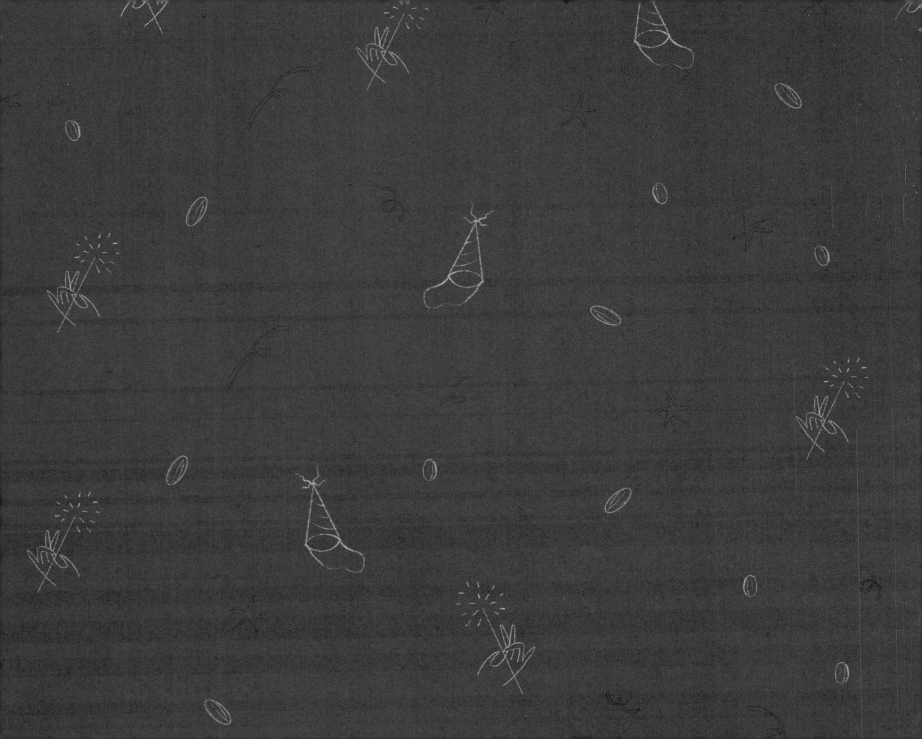